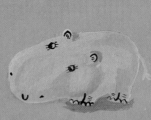

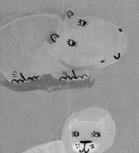

RubY
AND THE MUDDY DOG

To David and
Diamond Jim

KINGFISHER
An imprint of Kingfisher Publications Plc
New Penderel House, 283-288 High Holborn, London WC1V 7HZ

First published in 2000
2 4 6 8 10 9 7 5 3 1
1TR/1299/TWP/HBM/15ONYMA

Text and illustrations copyright © Helen Stephens 2000

A CIP catalogue record for this book is available from the British Library.

ISBN 0 7534 0401 X

Printed in Singapore

RubY and the MUDDY DOG

Helen Stephens

KINGFISHER

"Hello," said Ruby.
"Hello," said Dog. "Can I come and live with you?"

"OK," said Ruby. "But be neat and tidy!"
"I will," said Dog.

Dog ran inside and into the
sitting-room.

"Who made these muddy pawprints?" said Ruby.

Dog blushed . . .

"Hippo did it!" he said.

"Hmm . . ." said Ruby. "You'd better go
and play in the garden."

"OK!" said Dog.

And he ran outside . . .

straight into the pond!

"Who spoilt my flowers?" said Ruby.

Dog blushed.
"Lion did it!" he said.

"Hmm . . ." said Ruby. "You'd better go inside and have a bath."
"OK," said Dog.

Dog ran to the bathroom and jumped into the bath.

He spilt banana bubble bath everywhere!

Dog tried to tidy up . . .

but he made it even worse!

"Who made this terrible mess?" shouted Ruby.

"Lion and Hippo did it," said Dog.

"We're fed up with being blamed,"
said Lion and Hippo. "We're leaving."

Poor Dog.
He didn't want his friends to leave.

"Sorry, Lion. Sorry, Hippo," said Dog.
"I didn't want to get into trouble."

"You don't have to tell big fibs," said Ruby.
"Sorry," said Dog. "I didn't think you'd let
me stay if I made a mess."

"We love you even if you are a bit clumsy,"
said Lion and Hippo.

"You can live with us for ever," said Ruby.
And she gave Dog a big hug.